THE STRIKE
AT SHANE'S

THE STRIKE AT SHANE'S

A SEQUEL TO "BLACK BEAUTY"

A PRIZE STORY OF INDIANA

APPLEWOOD BOOKS
BEDFORD, MASSACHUSETTS

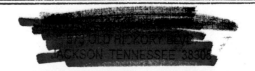

The Strike at Shane's was originally published in 1893 by the American Humane Education Society.

Thank you for purchasing an Applewood Book. Applewood reprints America's lively classics—books from the past that are of interest to modern readers. For a free copy of our current catalog, write to: Applewood Books, P.O. Box 365, Bedford, MA 01730.

10 9 8 7 6 5 4 3 2 1

ISBN 1-55709-308-3

Library of Congress Catalog Card Number: 99-62288

THE STRIKE AT SHANE'S.

CHAPTER I.

EE up, there, Dobbin! Whoop!" With a shout that rang through the forest Tom Shane let the heavy "black snake" whip fall on the flanks of the two willing horses. Again and again the heavy whip fell on the "*off*" horse, which was apparently unable to "pull even" with the *younger horse* on the "near" side. The horses tugged at the traces, and floundered about in the mud, but were unable to move the heavy load to which they were hitched.

"Be aisy there now, Tom, will ye? It's stuck ye are now, sure enough," said an Irishman who came up just then.

"It's all on account of that lazy Dobbin," said Tom, "he didn't pull a pound."

"Arrah, there now, it's forgettin' the age o' the horse ye are. *Sure, there wasn't a horse on the place could pull wid him whin he was younger.* It's gettin' along in the years I am mesilf, an' age will be wearin' the strength o' a horse the same as a man. Let 'em stand 'til I get a bit of a pry under the wheel."

He procured a fence rail, and proceeded to put it under the wheel as a lever to lift it a little out of the "chuck hole" where it had stopped. Those who are familiar with the ungravelled roads of Indiana in former years need not be told what a "chuck hole" is; but to those not experienced in such matters it might be explained that heavy hauling over these roads will wear deep holes with sharp edges, and when the wheel of a loaded wagon drops into one of these holes it is very difficult to pull it out. Thanks to an increased population, such roads are not so numerous as they were in former years, and teaming is not necessarily such a horse-killing business as it used to be.

"Now, will ye give 'em another pull?" said Mike, who had his "bit of a pry" under the wheel, and was dangling on the end of it doing his best to lift the wheel a little.

"Give 'em a schmall taste of the whip, to encourage 'em a little," he cried.

Again the whip was unsparingly used by Tom, and the two horses exerted all their powers, but only succeeded in moving the wagon enough to let Mike's pry slip out, and he came sprawling down in the mud. But more serious results had followed. Old Dobbin was down, and Tom, in his anger, was cutting him with his whip to make him get up.

"Hould on there, bye," shouted Mike, coming forward, covered with mud. "Ye wouldn't sthrike a man whin he's down; thin why don't ye show the same dacency to a dumb brute! Unhitch the chains there; don't you see the ould horse is chokin'?"

"Little do I care if he dies," said Tom, as he ungraciously assisted in extricating him. "Here it is comin' night, an' this load stuck here in the middle of the road all on account of that old brute."

"It's the fault o' yer feyther, it is; for if he'd be doin' the right thing by old Dobbin he'd give 'im the run o' the pasture for the rist of his days widout a bit of work to do. It's goin' on twinty years since he was broke to the harness, an' that's afore you was borned," said Mike.

"Come, old fellow, get up;" and he assisted the old horse to his feet.

"Hello, there, what's up?" shouted the driver of a team that had come up behind.

"Sure, an' it's stuck in the mud we are," said Mike. "An' it's glad we are to see ye, Mr. Tracy, if ye'll give us a pull at the ind o' the tongue wid thim beautiful horses o' yourn."

"Ah, it's Shane's team!" said Mr. Tracy, "and old Dobbin has been down. Shane never will learn when a horse is used up. He's had twenty years good service out of that horse and isn't satisfied yet. That's a good load for four horses over such roads as these."

"That's thrue," said Mike, "*but Shane niver sinds four horses to do the work he can get out of two.*"

Mr. Tracy's team was soon hitched to the end of the tongue, and the four horses easily pulled the wagon out of the mud.

"The old horse is winded," said Mr. Tracy, "and can never pull that load home. It's a shame to treat a faithful old horse in that manner. You had better pull out to the side of the road, and come back in the morning with a better team."

Mr. Tracy's advice was taken, as it was evident that old Dobbin was about used up.

About twenty-five years previous to this time John Shane had moved to Indiana, and had bought a small farm, on which he built a saw mill; and by running the mill in winter and farming in summer he had added to his possessions until he was now the owner of two hundred acres of fine farm land. He had been a hard-working man, and was now considered a well-equipped and prosperous farmer. He was a hard man to deal with, and always aimed to make a dollar where other people made a dime.

It was a favorite maxim of his that nothing should stay on the farm that did not more than pay expenses.

There was not a beast or fowl on the farm but what his careful eye was on it, and everything must bring in money or its fate was sealed.

Avarice held full sway over his mind, and there was no room in his nature for kindness. Everything on the place felt the effects of his ill-temper — even his family did not always escape. His son Tom had, to a great degree, absorbed his father's sentiments, although a good boy at heart. A boy's character is often ruined by his early training, and Tom was guilty of many acts of cruelty to dumb animals which he did not know were wrong, simply because his father had set him that kind of example. He did not know that he was violating any rule of humanity by such acts, because his thoughts had not been directed in that channel.

Altogether the animals on Shane's farm had a pretty hard time of it. There were two redeeming characters on the farm, however, and they were Mrs. Shane and her daughter Edith. Invariably kind and gentle in their ways, they were loved by everything on the farm, and their righteous indignation would sometimes get the better of their judgment, and they would speak their minds about the cruelties practised by father and son. They would usually meet with the reply that "Women had better keep still about things that don't consarn 'em." And John Shane said, "Nothin' made him madder than for a woman to interfere when he was dealin' with his animals."

Tom, having arrived at home, and put the horses in the stable, came into the house, just as the family were sitting down to the supper table.

"You are late to-night, Tom," said Shane. "Has anything gone wrong?"

"Yes, everything's gone wrong," answered Tom, in a surly mood; "and if I can't have a better team to work with I won't do any more teamin'."

"Come, sir," said his father, "none of that kind of talk—I won't have it. What's the matter with the team?"

"Why, enough's the matter," said Tom. "We got stuck in the mud down by Ford's, an' old Dobbin choked down an' would'nt pull a pound;" and Tom proceeded to tell the whole affair as it occurred, not omitting Mr. Tracy's remarks.

"I think Tracy had better mind his own business and leave mine alone," said Shane, a little piqued.

"Well, if he had, your wagon would be standing down there in a mud hole yet," said Tom.

"That ain't what I mean," said Shane. "That's no more than I'd do for a neighbor; but I know a good horse as well as Tracy does; an' my horses don't take no back seat for his neither."

"He don't drive any wind-broken nor worn-out horses," retorted Tom.

"No more would I if it wasn't for your mother, who makes me keep old Dobbin."

"Well, John," said Mrs. Shane, mildly, "*you don't need to work old Dobbin* if you do keep him. I am sure, as Mr. Tracy says, he has earned a rest for the balance of his life."

"You know my principles, Mary, that nothin' shall stay on this farm that don't pay expenses."

"*I brought Dobbin here when I married you, John, and here he is going to stay as long as he lives.*"

Something in the tone of her voice touched a chord in John Shane's heart that caused his memory to turn back to the time when he married Mary. He was kind-hearted and happy then — but oh, those times were different. A man could'nt afford to be generous now or the world would get the best of him. But why?

"An' I say, father," said Tom, breaking in, "if

mother insists on keeping Dobbin, let's turn him out to pasture. It won't cost much to keep him, an' I won't drive a broken-down horse for people to make remarks about."

"Especially Cora Tracy's father," said Edith.

"No, not 'especially' anybody," said Tom, bridling up, but blushing at the same time.

"Well, we'll see about it," said Shane. "I don't want to hear any more about it to-night."

Thus he put the matter off, hoping that the event would be forgotten by morning, and that nothing more would be said about it.

CHAPTER II.

HE events just told took place in the early spring, just at the time when the spring work was commencing on the farm. The trees were beginning to put forth their leaves, and the meadows and fields were green with the growing grass. The violets along the fence rows were turning up their little faces to the warm sun, and every bird familiar to the climate had made its appearance. Their joyous songs rang through the woods as they flitted hither and thither, building their nests, or turning over the leaves looking for bugs and worms. There was no ill-temper displayed by these dwellers of the forest as they went about their work, seeking a living, or building their nests for the summer. Why should not the human family go about their work just as joyously as the birds of the forest?

> "Whistle and hoe, sing as you go,
> Shorten the row by the songs you know."

No such an idea as this had ever entered John Shane's head, for with him everything was bustle and hurry.

The day broke bright and clear on the morning after Dobbin's misfortune, and the Shane household was up with the sun to begin their daily duties. The conversation of the previous evening had been forgotten by Shane — or at least thrust into the background by more important matters; and as he hurried to the barn to look after the feeding, his only thought was how to get the most work done that day. He walked down the row of stalls, throwing corn into the feed boxes, until he came to Dobbin's stall, when he stopped as though thunderstruck. Old Dobbin was standing with his head down, wheezing like a man with the asthma.

"Hello; here's a fine go, right in the busy season. Just my everlastin' bad luck!" he exclaimed, for the appearance of Dobbin indicated a severe case of lung fever.

Shane never gave any thought to the comfort of his animals, and Tom followed in the footsteps of his father. He had brought Dobbin home wet with sweat, and tied him in his stall without rubbing him down, and such a thing as a blanket was never heard of in Shane's stables. Tom's ill temper had made him even forget to put in the usual bedding of clean straw, and the result was, as any good horseman might expect, that Dobbin had taken a severe cold.

"How now, Tom," cried Shane, as Tom entered the barn, "here's a nice mess you've made of things."

Tom stood with his hands in his pockets, staring at Dobbin; and while his conscience compelled him to feel a little sympathy for the old horse's sufferings, yet he had the secret satisfaction of knowing that he would not have to drive him any more for a few days, anyhow.

"You go down to town an' bring up Hodges, an' see what he can do for him," said Shane.

Had he known what would be the result of this action, he would rather have said, "You take him down to the woods an' put a bullet in his brain." But he thought Hodges could doctor the old horse up so that he would be able to work again.

Shane got Dobbin out of the stable in the meantime, although he was so stiff he could scarcely walk.

Hodges, the veterinary surgeon, soon came and said he thought he could cure him, but that he didn't believe he would ever be worth much, or able to do much hard work again.

"Well, I'll spend no money on him," said Shane. "Here's your fee for this time, and you needn't come any more."

"*Mr. Hodges,*" said a voice behind them, "*you can give old Dobbin all the attention he needs, and I will see that you are paid.*" It was Mrs. Shane, who had come up just in time to hear Shane's last remark.

Shane growled out something about "squandering money," and turning on his heel, went to the barn.

Hodges left medicine with Mrs. Shane, and she and Edith got the old horse into the yard and wrapped him up in an old quilt. They bathed his limbs with the ointment left by Hodges, and Mrs. Shane held his mouth open while Edith poured in the medicine for him to swallow.

Dobbin's condition soon became known throughout the barnyard, and also the cause of it. There is no question but animals do have some means of communicating with each other. How it is done we do not know. *All migratory birds and fowls have a public meeting before starting on their journeys southward, and go in flocks.* It is interesting to watch a public gathering of crows, and see the dignified manner in which they will carry on the meeting until there arises a difference of opinion on some point, and then there commences such a chattering and cawing, and rising to points of order, or for personal explanation, as was never heard outside of a session of congress. But in the end they always come to some kind of a decision — *which congress does not always do.*

It is said that the eagles of southern Indiana have a place of meeting where they hold an annual gathering, and make an apportionment of the country, assigning to each pair a certain territory over which they may hunt; and this meeting of eagles has never been known to be *guilty of making a gerrymander*, thereby setting a good example to some of our legislatures. It is not necessary for me to enumerate the many acts of sagacity of our domestic animals to show that they have some means of communicating ideas from one to the other.

Old Dobbin was a favorite with everything on the farm, and the news of his misfortune spread in a short time, and was a matter of general discussion by all the animals. Even the chickens missed him, for he never objected to their eating a few grains of corn out of his box; but if they got in his way he would push them gently aside with his nose.

Even John Shane missed him, but it was the result of a selfish interest; for here was his team broken up, and not a horse on the place to take his place. There was no use of talking about breaking one of the colts; and *Bay Dick had such a temper* that he couldn't be worked with any horse *but Dobbin*. If he should hitch one of the colts up with Dick, everything would be kicked to splinters in five minutes.

He went among his neighbors and tried to hire or buy a horse, but it was the busy season, and none of them cared to part with any of their horses. In this way he spent the whole day and succeeded in doing nothing but get into a very bad temper.

He went down to the field where Mike was plowing with the only team on the farm, and told him not to spare the horses, but "put 'em through from daylight till dark."

"*Not if I know mesilf*," said Mike to himself, as Shane started away. "It's not such a fool I am to overtax me own stringth for the sake of getting a little more work out of the horses."

Shane searched far and wide for a horse, but could find none at that season of the year. His temper grew worse all the time. Tom didn't escape his wrath either; but Tom had a way of getting even by taking out his spite on the cattle and horses, and even the dog and cat did not entirely escape his kicks and blows. And his leisure time was spent going about the fields shooting birds, as he said "for practise."

Things went on this way for a week or ten days,

when Shane concluded to try breaking one of the colts. *His idea of breaking a colt was by force*, and the thought never entered his head that he could subdue it by gentleness. The strong-limbed, beautiful colt was enticed into the stable, and the door securely fastened. A rope with a slip-noose was then thrown over its head, and as it plunged away the rope tightened around its neck until it was choked almost into insensibility. A strong bridle was then placed on it and the noose was loosened. After being pulled around and whipped for about an hour the colt became too much exhausted to make further resistance, and Shane held it by the bit while Tom fitted on the collar and harness. Bay Dick was then brought out and hitched to the wagon, and the colt was placed alongside of him. Dick resented the idea of being hitched with a colt, and evinced some restlessness. "Gettin' frisky, are you?" said Shane, and he gave Dick a cut with the whip which raised a long welt on his side.

Dick laid back his ears, as much as to say, "I'll get even with you for that."

"All ready; let go!" shouted Shane, and Tom released the colt's head, which he had been holding by the bit. It began to rear and plunge about in its efforts to get loose. Dick caught the excitement of the moment, and began plunging and kicking with all his might. The team then started to run, dragging Shane a short distance, when he let go,— and they sped down the lane like a hurricane. The wagon was torn to pieces, and the two horses, trying to jump a fence, went down together, and were tangled up in the harness. Shane and Tom hastened to the place and extricated them. Dick was all right, *but the colt's leg was broken.*

"Go to the house and get the rifle," said Shane.

Tom went; and when he came back Shane put a bullet in the colt's head, saying, "It's no use to fool with a colt with a broken leg."

Such are the sentiments of many whose hearts are closed against the silent appeals of our dumb animals.

How often have we seen the look of pain in a horse's eye after receiving cruel blows for failing to do what was impossible — *a look which almost seemed to say, "God forgive them, for they know not what they do!"*

CHAPTER III.

NDER the kind treatment of Mrs. Shane Dobbin had improved rapidly, and was able to be turned out in the pasture; but he was still stiff in the joints and short in his wind. Shane had succeeded in getting a man from the village to come with his team and work a few days, but he was far behind his neighbors in getting his corn planted. This soured his temper more than anything else, for he was always ahead of his neighbors in his work, and he blamed it all to "his everlastin' bad luck."

From this time on he hardly gave his horses time to eat and sleep, and they were worked down almost to skin and bone. Dick's temper had not improved any, and he bore the marks of the whip frequently; for Shane said the only way to control a horse was to make him fear you.

About this time it became known about the farm that Dobbin had called a meeting of all the animals on the farm to take some measures for the amelioration of their condition. This meeting was to be held on the next Sunday, as that was the only day when the horses could get off.

Now, the animals did not know exactly what was to be done at the meeting; but they had great confidence in Dobbin, and attended the meeting in full force. It was held under the old oak tree down in the pasture beside the brook. The gathering was rather a surprise to Dobbin, for he had not expected so many. He had given notice that all the useful animals and fowls of the farm should be present, and as the result all the horses, cattle, sheep and swine were there, and all the chickens, turkeys, ducks and geese had sent representatives. Towser, the dog, and puss, the cat, were there in person. All the birds of the forest had sent representatives, and there were also representatives from the snakes and toads.

It was with some apprehension that Dobbin took charge of this great gathering, as it was the first time he had ever attempted to preside over a public meeting, and he would have found himself afflicted with a trembling of the knees if his knees had not been too stiff to tremble. More than that, he was doubtful if all the representatives present were entitled to seats in the convention; but he concluded to take the matter in his own hands without appointing a committee on credentials — probably owing to the fact that he never heard of such a committee. He concluded to take the most difficult problem under consideration first, and called on the snakes and toads to state their claims to sit in the convention.

"We are not animals," said one of the toads, "neither are we fowls; but we do claim to be useful. We destroy many noxious insects that would injure the crops grown on the farm. In fact, we live entirely on insects — such as flies, roaches, mosquitoes, worms, and bugs, that would destroy agricultural crops. And we have been treated " —

" Never mind how you have been treated," said Dobbin, "we will hear that further on. I believe your statements to be true, and will allow you to remain in the convention."

" And we," said one of the snakes, "live on insects the same as the toad, and assist in protecting the crops from these pests."

" Yes," said the toad, "you sometimes make a meal on one of my species."

"I admit that such things have been done, but I have never been guilty of such a crime," said the snake.

" Is not your bite poisonous, and are you not a dangerous fellow to have about?" inquired Dobbin.

" An entirely mistaken idea," said the snake ; "*there is but one poisonous snake in the State, and that is the rattle-snake.* We do not associate with them at all. Although our teeth are sharp, we have no poison fangs, and our bite is no more dangerous than the prick of a needle. For the proof of this I refer you to any scientific investigator of the age."

" Well, we will accept your statements as true, and allow you to remain in the convention," said Dobbin.

" Bravo !" shouted some one in the rear, and Dobbin looked around and saw a long-eared mule.

" Hello ! by what right are you here?" inquired **Dobbin.**

"By the right of my ability to get here," said the mule. "I am at present a free and independent character in this community, and seeing you assembled here I thought I would come over and see what the caucus was about."

"May I ask where you belong?" inquired Dobbin.

"I was formerly employed by a street car company of Indianapolis. I received too many kicks and blows and too much hard work for the amount of food I got, so I escaped from the stables and came out in the country for a vacation," said the mule.

"Well," said Dobbin, "if you stay *here* you will not be likely to find your condition any better."

"Never mind about me," said the mule. "It's just as easy to jump out of the field as it was to jump in; and if farmer Shane tries to capture me, he'll find I'm something of a kicker."

"That may be," said Dobbin, "but you will find that farmer Shane is something of a kicker too, as all the animals on the farm can testify."

"We will now proceed with the business of the meeting," said Dobbin, "and will call on all the assembled company to state their grievances and make suggestions for the remedy."

The cow was called upon.

"My troubles are not as serious as those of some others on the farm; but I don't think I have been treated fairly," said the cow. "I give all the milk for the family, and don't begrudge them any of it, yet *when they took my calf from me* I couldn't help but worry about it, and once I jumped the fence to get to it. Then Tom came with a club and beat me, and set Towser on me. I don't think that Towser is a bit better than Tom."

"Mr. Chairman, I want to say a word here," said Towser, coming forward. "I admit that I have chased all the cattle, horses and hogs on the farm; but I have to do what my master commands me to do, for if I don't I will get kicks and blows. I haven't inflicted any serious injury on any of you, for my bark has always been worse than my bite."

"We must not always judge each other by our actions," said Dobbin, "for we are sometimes compelled to do things that we would not do if left to our own free wills."

"More than that," continued the cow, "that good-for-nothing Tom beats me and kicks me when he comes to milk me. He puts my neck in a stall where I can't turn my head around, and if I switch my tail to keep the flies off he gets mad and beats me. Why, last night he tied my tail to my leg so that I could not switch the flies, and a fly got on my back and bit me terribly. I couldn't switch it off with my tail, nor scare it off with my head. I stood it as long as I could, and then I kicked up with both of my feet. I only aimed to scare the fly away, but some way I kicked Tom over and spilled the bucket of milk all over him, and I'm carrying the bruises on me where he beat me for it. I don't give down my milk very well sometimes, but what encouragement is there for a cow that is treated in that manner?"

When the cow had finished, *Bay Dick* was called on.

"I don't intend to stand this treatment any longer," said Dick. "A horse don't get anything but blows on this farm, whether he does right or wrong. I know I've got a fiery temper, and always aim to take my own part. I'm sorry I ran away the other day and broke the colt's leg, but that's done and can't be helped. But one thing is certain, I don't intend to submit to this treatment any longer."

The other horses all said "bravo," and "that's right."

"I'd be willing to do my share of the work if I was treated right," he continued; "but I get nothing but kicks and cuffs, and never a kind word. And there's that Tom has been driving me every Sunday night down to Tracy's place. He ties me to a strong post out in the road, *with my head pulled away back with the check-rein*, so that I can't get my head down to rest it. Then he goes into the house *and stays until ten or eleven o'clock, while I stand there and shiver with the cold.* If he would just put a blanket over me I wouldn't suffer so much; but it's little he ever thinks of our comfort. I tried to break loose and come home, but I couldn't. You all know what old Dobbin has suffered at their hands, and that's what we'll all come to in the end."

This speech was indorsed by them all.

"I don't know that I have any grievance to speak of," said a pig. "I have a pretty good time. It's true I sometimes get through a hole in the fence, and then Towser —

"There it goes again," said Towser. "Always blaming me for something I can't help."

"As I said," continued the pig, "I haven't much to complain of, but if I can do anything to help the rest of you I will do it."

"There's a hole in the garden fence where my chickens would get in last summer, and then I would have to go in and watch them," said a hen. Then some of the other hens would get in, and Tom would come and throw stones at us. He killed two of my chickens and broke my wing. Sometimes he would set Towser on us—"

"There now, I won't stand it any longer," said Towser, bristling up.

"Order, order!" shouted Dobbin; and Towser lay down again.

"I'm kicked and cuffed day in and day out," mewed Puss. "I try to catch all the rats and mice I can, but it don't do any good."

"Am I allowed to speak?" asked a quail which had hopped up on the fence.

"What reason can you give for appearing in this meeting," asked Dobbin.

"For the reason that I live on insects, and bugs, and worms, which would be destructive to the farmer's crops. I speak for all classes of birds. It is true that we eat a little fruit and grain, but that is nothing in comparison to the great benefits the farmer receives from us. We have added greatly to the prosperity of the farm, yet our nests are destroyed, our young killed,

and the merciless guns of both Shane and his son are
popping away at us all the time."

"That being the case, all birds that destroy trouble-
some insects are admitted to the convention," said
Dobbin.

There being no more speakers, Dobbin said the convention would take a recess for five minutes, and go
down to the brook and get a drink, after which they
would discuss the matter as to the best and most con-
venient remedy for the evils existing on the farm.

CHAPTER IV.

HE meeting having re-assembled, Dobbin called for suggestions as to the proper remedy for their misfortunes, and the proper course to pursue. All were silent but *Bay Dick*, who was in favor of kicking everything to pieces on the farm, and to show how it was to be done he wheeled around and kicked the top rail off the fence.

"If you will allow me to make a suggestion," said the mule, "perhaps I could give you some ideas on this subject."

"We will hear what you have to say," said Dobbin.

"I have been in the service of the street car company for several years," said the mule, "and I know when the street car drivers got dissatisfied with their wages they went on a strike. That is, they quit work until their difficulties were fixed up in some way, and they got what they wanted. I know we mules had an easy time of it while the strike lasted. Now, why couldn't you all go out on a strike and refuse to work until you get better treatment?"

"That would probably result in more blows and worse treatment instead of better," said Dobbin.

"No," said the mule, "if farmer Shane had to do without you for a while he would perhaps begin to appreciate your services, and would come to his senses and treat you better."

After some further discussion this plan grew in favor and was adopted, and the mule which had been in the street car strike gave them full instructions how to proceed.

"I'll not do another day's work," said Dick, "and I'll kick everything to pieces they hitch me to."

"Hold on there," said the mule, "no violence to persons or property. That was the rule in the street car strike. Just quit work and let farmer Shane get along the best he can."

"That's right," said Dobbin, "no violence in this strike."

"Well, I'll do the best I can to keep cool," said Dick, "but they mustn't push me too far."

"Now, we will hear from each member as to the course they intend to pursue," said Dobbin.

"As for my part," said Dick, who was highly delighted with the plan, "I shall pretend to be very lame, and stiff in my shoulders."

"Considering your high temper," said the mule, "perhaps it would be better for you to locate your lameness in your hind legs."

"Not much," said Dick, "I may have occasion to use my heels before I get through this if they use me too severely."

"I shall stay in the farthest corner of the pasture,

and make Tom come after me every night instead of going up to the barn to be milked, as I have always done," said the cow, "and I shall give just as little milk as possible."

The other horses all agreed to feign some kind of sickness to avoid work.

"I will not do anything that I can get out of," said Towser, "if I have to chase any of you, you needn't get scared, for I'll not hurt you. There is one thing that I have always done, and that is, kill the moles in the yard and garden. They burrow under the ground, where puss can't get at them, and I have always made it a point to watch for them and kill them. I will not kill another mole if they destroy all the garden."

"I will not kill another rat or mouse on the farm, if they eat up all the grain," said Puss.

"Thank you for that," said a big rat, that came up out of a fence corner, where he had been hiding and listening.

"I want you to understand that it is not out of any consideration or respect I have for you that I made that statement," said Puss, and she walked over towards the rat, who immediately dropped back into his hole.

"Quite right and proper," said Dobbin; "we want no such characters in this convention."

The snake and toad said they would move over to the next farm.

"I shall move off the farm just as soon as my mate gets well of a wound received the other day from a

shot from Shane's gun," said the quail, " and I promise you that no quail shall come on this farm this
summer."

" I have a grievance against farmer Shane myself,"
said a hawk, that had perched unseen on the top of the
oak, " and I will agree to kill all the chickens on the
farm."

" Put him out! put him out!" screamed the hen;
and the other birds quickly sought cover.

" I'll fix him," said the kingbird, and he made a
quick dash at the hawk, and struck him in the back
with his sharp beak.

" I'll help," said the crow; and between them they
soon drove the hawk away.

" I spend almost the whole of my time catching
worms and bugs," chirped the robin.   " It is true,
that is the way I make my living, but those worms
would destroy many dollars' worth of crops.   Last
summer almost my whole family was killed by Shane
because we took a few cherries, and I promise you
there shall not a robin remain on the farm nor catch a
worm on it this summer."

So said all the birds; and it was then and there
arranged that there should be a general emigration of
birds from the Shane farm.

" Am I in this?" asked the crow, who had returned
from driving the hawk away, which he had chased
clear over to the adjoining farm.

"Well, that's questionable," said Dobbin. But owing
to the fact that the crow had chased away the hawk,

Dobbin was disposed to look more kindly on him than he otherwise would.

" Ah! you black rogue," said the hen, " you stole an egg out of my nest yesterday. I saw you fly away with it."

" I admit it," said the crow; " but I drove away a rat that was just about to steal it, and I thought I might take the egg as a reward for driving the rat away. Besides, I drive away hawks which would steal chickens, and I kill a great many grubworms, and cutworms, and ground mice," continued the crow, " and if I'm a part of this strike I'll not kill any more such pests, and more than that, I'll move off the farm and let the hawks kill all Shane's chickens."

" Oh! come now," said the hen, " let's compromise; you stay here and keep the hawks away, and I'll give you an egg now and then."

" All right," said the crow; " I'll agree to anything to get into good society."

" I have a few words to say," said the blackbird; " I'm black like the crow, but I don't steal eggs."

" Yes; but I saw you pulling up corn down in the field yesterday, which is just as bad," said Dobbin.

" Quite mistaken, I assure you," said the blackbird. Sometimes I pull up a sprout of corn, but it is to get at the grubworm which is at the root. If I did not pull it up the grub would destroy it anyhow, so in the end no harm is done by me, but much good, for I destroy a worm that would have destroyed many stalks of corn before the season is over. We cannot destroy all the grubworms and cutworms that are in the corn-fields, for they are under ground and we cannot get at them. We follow the plow in the spring and get all the worms that it turns up. We follow in the summer and get all the worms that the cultivator brings to the surface. Thousands of crickets and grasshoppers are destroyed by us which would injure the wheat and grass crops. Hundreds of my species have been killed by Shane, and I will promise you that not a worm nor an insect shall be killed by a blackbird on the farm this summer. More than that, all the blackbirds in this section will join me, and each one will carry a few grubworms and cutworms and drop them on Shane's fields."

Dobbin thought that carrying worms on the farm for the purpose of destroying the crops was contrary to the arrangement that no violence should be done to the person or property of Shane; but the birds all insisted that it was no more than right that they should have this privilege. They thought that was the best way to prove to Shane the great amount of damage done by these pests.

Everything being now arranged, the convention adjourned to meet again on the following Sunday at the same place, and report what had been done.

"*Wonder what all them beasts are gathered around that tree for?*" said Shane, as he and Tom sauntered across the field, laying their plans for the next day's work. "Must be somethin' wrong."

"They're just standin' in the shade of that tree, I

guess," answered Tom; "but it does seem kind of strange, for there's Towser among 'em, an' he don't often go very far away from the house."

"Yes, an' there's some other critter there, too, that don't belong to this farm," said Shane.

"It's a mule," said Tom. "I wonder where in the nation he came from?"

Shane and Tom having come close enough for the animals to see them, the mule started across the field to the point where he had jumped the fence. Towser, seeing the turn affairs had taken, started after the mule, as though chasing it, and made a bee-line for home as soon as he was out of sight of Shane. The other animals scattered in various directions, and Shane and Tom proceeded in the direction the mule had taken to see where it had gotten in.

CHAPTER V.

ONDAY morning came bright and fair, and Shane was up at dawn. He fed the horses, and seeing the sorrel horse lying down, he thought the horse was still sleeping, and threw a corncob at him.

"Come, wake up there, lazy bones," he shouted, but the only response was a groan.

"What in the nation is the matter now?" he asked himself, as he went around in the stable and gave the horse a poke with the fork handle.

"Get up here," he shouted, and gave the horse another poke with the fork handle. The sorrel got up on his feet, but stood with his head down.

"He'd better not try that with me," said Dick, to himself, in an undertone, as he munched his corn.

"Looks like a sick horse, sure," said Shane. "I never knew that horse to refuse to eat before. Fire and thunder!" he exclaimed, as he looked in the gray mare's stall, and saw that she had not touched her corn. "Somebody must have poisoned these horses."

He led the sorrel horse and gray mare out in the barn-yard, where they rolled around and made a great show of having the colic.

"Tom, come here!" shouted Shane, as Tom came

sauntering down the path with his milk pail. "You put the saddle on Dick, an' go down an' get Hodges as quick as you can."

Tom did as he was commanded; but when he attempted to bring Dick out of the stable he pretended to be so stiff that he could not get out. Shane was called up and made acquainted with the state of affairs.

"What in the nation do you suppose is the matter with 'em?" he asked, still more astounded. "'Tain't no founder, for they haven't been overfed."

"I've an idea that it's some of that mule's work," said Tom. "Like as not he's been kicked."

"I reckon one mule wouldn't kick all the horses on the place," said Shane, as they examined him for hoof marks and found none.

"Well, you'll just have to walk down to town an' get Hodges, an' be quick about it."

"It does beat all," said Shane, as he returned to the house. "There's no misfortune flyin' that don't 'light on this farm."

"What is the matter now?" asked Mrs. Shane.

"Why, every horse on the farm is disabled in one way or another," said Shane.

"Well, I thought you were working those horses too hard," said Mrs. Shane. "You should remember, John, that horses are not machines that can go on forever. You should judge their feelings something by your own. You raised Mike's wages for working over time, *but what have you given these horses for their overwork?* Have you given them any better care or better food?"

"Oh, you have foolish notions about such things, an' you and me will never agree on them pints," said Shane.

"It is true, nevertheless, that if you would give your horses better care, and lighter work, you would be the gainer in the end," said Mrs. Shane.

"How can I help it," said Shane; "here's only three horses left on the farm, an' I've got to get all the work I can out of 'em."

"It was overwork that put Dobbin in the shape he is now in," said Mrs. Shane. "If he had been properly cared for, and not been given work he couldn't do, he would have worked all summer."

"Well, what's done can't be undone; an' I've got to get them horses on their feet again. Them foolish notions of yours won't make any money on the farm; so there's no use discussin' 'em."

"Time will show," was Mrs. Shane's parting shot.

Hodges soon arrived, and worked on the horses all day, and at night they did not seem any better than when he began. He said they were the most peculiar and stubborn cases he had ever seen. Dick had several quiet laughs at the expense of the other horses because they had to take nasty medicine, while his treatment was external. Hodges said he couldn't see what was the matter with the horses, unless their constitutions were entirely broken down by overwork. He left in the evening with instructions that if the horses were not better by morning to let him know.

"Did you see that big flock of blackbirds down in

the lower field," inquired Shane of Tom at the supper table that evening.

"Yes," said Tom; "there must have been hundreds of 'em."

"You must get out early with the shot-gun in the mornin,' or there won't be a grain of corn left in the ground."

"Mr. Tracy says that blackbirds do more good than harm," said Edith. "He says that all birds destroy bugs and worms."

"Tracy has got lots of fool notions in his head that there ain't any money in," said Shane.

"Well, I think it's cruel to shoot birds that don't know they are doing any harm. I'm sure you wouldn't want to be shot for doing something that you didn't know was wrong," replied Edith.

The further discussion of the matter was postponed by Shane, who said he had more serious things to think about.

"Mornin' to ye, Tom," said Mike, as he met Tom in the lane, gun in hand, bent on destroying blackbirds.

"What be ye goin' to shoot this mornin'?"

"Blackbirds," replied Tom.

"Begorra, there's plinty of 'em," said Mike.

"It looks like I would get a chance to use my gun," said Tom.

"Thim's quare birds, now, Tom. I was watchin' 'em yisterday an' begorra, do ye know, I think they're plantin' corn instid o' takin' it up; for I see 'em a droppin' somethin' white all over the field, and there be hundreds of 'em at it. But how is thim horses this mornin'?"

"No better; an' the old man is as mad as a hornet," said Tom, as he passed on down the lane in search of blackbirds. There was abundance of them, and Tom thought he would have fine sport killing them, but they were on the alert, and not a bird did he succeed in killing, although he tramped around the fields until he was tired out.

"Tom, you surely didn't milk that cow dry," said Mrs. Shane; "you didn't get half as much milk as you usually do."

"She wouldn't give down her milk," said Tom. "The old brute needed a good beating — and she got it, too."

"You must not ill-treat that cow," said Mrs. Shane. "Nothing will ruin a good cow as soon as cruel treatment. If you won't treat the cow right I will have to do the milking myself."

"It ain't my fault that she is so mean," said Tom, as he walked out in the yard, and discovering a bird's nest in the cedar tree, picked up a long pole and began to punch at it, when Edith came out and saw him.

"Tom Shane, what are you doing?" she cried; "you leave that bird's nest alone."

"I won't," he said. "It's a nasty old robin's nest, and I don't want 'em here."

"They don't hurt anything, and do lots of good, and sing so nice."

"They steal cherries, and don't do any good," said Tom; "an' who cares for their singin'?"

"I do, and Cora Tracy does, and so does mamma. Cora and I watched them building that nest day before yesterday. They didn't come back to-day; and I believe you have done something to them. I'll tell Cora if you tear it down," she said, as Tom made another vigorous punch at the nest.

"Don't care if you do," said Tom, as he gave another punch at the tree with his pole; but he was careful, however, not to strike the nest, and laid down his pole and walked away. Tom was just at the age when the influence of the gentler sex was most powerful over him, and he hesitated to do anything that might bring him into disfavor with Cora Tracy.

"Oh! mamma, do come here and see," cried Edith, the next day, as she was walking around in the yard. "The moles have eaten up all the tulips."

Mrs. Shane came out to see the wreck of her beautiful tulip bed.

"Here, Towser! come and hunt the moles," called Mrs. Shane to Towser, who lay on the porch. He came down slowly and walked up to Mrs. Shane, and licked her hand. He then started down the path, barking as though he saw some one.

"Here, Towser! come back now, and hunt the moles." Towser came back, and Mrs. Shane pointed to the burrow and told him to hunt, but he hung his head and walked away.

"Why, what ails the dog?" said Mrs. Shane, "I never saw him act so."

"Towser, you naughty dog," cried Edith, "why

don't you mind?''—but Towser was gone. He remem-
bered his promise, and kept it, but he felt so mean that
he went around in the back yard and growled at Tom,
until he received a kick, and then he felt better.

The next day the pigs were in the garden, and Edith
called Towser to run them out. He lay still with his
nose between his paws, and apparently paid no attention to her.

"You naughty, lazy dog. You shall not have any
supper for that," cried Edith, as she went after the
pigs.

CHAPTER VI.

N the following Sunday the beasts and birds of the Shane farm met at the appointed place under the oak tree. Some of them looked rather the worse for the past week's experience; but all had a determined air, and looked willing to add a little more to the usual amount of suffering, if it would assist them in bettering their condition.

Dobbin called the meeting to order and stated that they would now hear from each one as to their experiences of the past week. Owing to the fact that Mrs. Shane had insisted that Dobbin should not be worked any more, he was an independent character on the farm. He had not been expected to work, and, as a consequence, had not been ill treated.

Bay Dick pranced forward, and said he was not so lame as he had been. "However, I am liable to be lame in good earnest if they give me much more of the treatment that I have received for the past week. I tell you it is hard to keep my heels down and not kick things to pieces. I haven't kicked any this week, though I don't promise for the future, for I have put up with about all the abuse I can stand without striking back."

"Keep cool," said Dobbin; "let us all work together and be patient."

"Patience is a virtue I don't boast of," said Dick;
"but I will do the best I can."

The sorrel said that playing sick was about as hard
as working, for he had been going hungry all the week,
a sick horse, of course, not being expected to eat.
He could get along all right as long as they would turn
him out in the pasture, where he could crop the grass
without being seen; but when they shut him up in the
stable they could tell how much he ate.

The gray mare had the same experience, but they
both promised to hold out to the end, if it took all
summer, and they got so thin that they had to stand
twice in the same place to make a shadow.

"I have had a pretty rough time of it," said the
cow. "The only way I could get even was by not
giving milk, and the only way I could keep from giving milk was not to eat. I have had to starve myself
for the whole week, but I have the satisfaction of knowing that they have not had enough milk in the family;
and that good-for-nothing Tom has not had any milk
to drink for one week. No doubt I am looking pretty
thin, but I am determined not to give any milk if I can
help it. I have received several beatings from Tom,
because he says I won't give down my milk, and I
kicked him once."

"That is quite heroic on your part," said Dobbin.
"Who is the next?"

"There never was a dog had as hard a time as I

do," said Towser. "I have tried not to do anything, but I get so many kicks and blows that I have to pretend to do something to keep them from beating me to death. By 'them' I mean Mr. Shane and Tom, for Mrs. Shane and Edith are as kind as they can be. I haven't killed a mole this week, and they ate up all of Mrs Shane's flowers. I was awfully sorry about that for I haven't anything against Mrs. Shane. And then when Edith told me to drive the hogs out of the garden I wouldn't go, and she had to go and drive them out herself. I licked her hand afterwards and tried to make up with her, but she wouldn't, and said I was a lazy dog. I'll make it all up to her when this strike is over."

"I just had to lay an egg every day," said the hen, "but I made a nest away back under the barn where they couldn't find it, and then went up in the hay-mow and cackled. I know they haven't found any eggs for they are all there, except what I gave the crow, and I think he earned them, for I haven't seen a hawk for a week."

"The rats and mice are about to take the place, for I haven't bothered them this week," said puss. "When I get hungry for a mouse, I go over to the next farm to get it. Shane said I ought to be starved into catching mice. Humph! there are mice to catch in other places than here. I won't starve."

"I have done my part," said the crow. "The hen has been giving me eggs to eat, and I have spent my spare time in carrying worms and dropping them on the fields, and I have had about a hundred of my friends at the same work. No wonder the hen has not seen a hawk this week, for no hawk will ever come around where a hundred crows are."

"You have no doubt seen the result of my work," said the blackbird. "I have had some hundreds of my friends at work carrying worms and insects on to the farm and dropping them. There will be enough worms on the farm within the next week to eat up all the crops this summer."

"I don't think that is right," said Dobbin, "for Shane may change his mind before the season is over, and then we would be sorry for what we have done."

"Oh! don't worry about that," said the blackbird. "I have explained the matter to them, and they have all agreed to assist in carrying all the worms and insects off again, if events should take a favorable turn for us. We'll make that all right."

"With that understanding, I consent that the work go on," said Dobbin.

"Tom has been chasing us all the week with his gun, but we keep out of his way. It's open war between us from now on, and we'll see which wins," said the blackbird.

The other birds said they had been engaged in similar work, and that there was not now a single bird of any kind on the farm.

While this meeting was going on, Shane had gone over to the Tracy farm to see if he could not get Mr. Tracy to help him out with his work.

"It seems like fate is agin me this year," said Shane. "What little crops I have got in are about to be taken by the birds. It keeps Tom all the time to keep 'em out of the corn."

"You and I have different views about such things," said Mr. Tracy. "*I consider the birds my best friends; I wouldn't part with them for any money, and I don't allow a bird shot on my farm.*"

"I never could see it in that light," said Shane. "I know they pull up the corn and there's enough blackbirds on my farm to take all the corn I can plant."

"Why, there's just as many on my farm and they follow the plow and pick up every worm and bug they can find. I'm satisfied that the work done for me this spring by blackbirds alone is worth fifty dollars to me, and they are not half done yet. I have a great deal more work for them to do for me before the season is over. Why, the birds are one of God's best gifts to us, and we ought to give Him thanks for sending them. They are not only a benefit to us in money, but their songs brighten our lives and make our homes more pleasant."

"I never have time to listen to their singin'," said Shane, "and as for their usefulness, I think they injure us more than they do us good."

"Well, I hope you will see things in a different light some time, and be able to understand what a good gift they are to us."

"I never can see things like you do," said Shane;

"an' it's no use for us to argy for we can't agree.
When luck begins to run agin a man there's no stoppin'
it. Now there's all them horses of mine disabled, an'
I don't know what to do."

"Now to be candid, friend Shane, don't you think you
are in a measure responsible for the condition of your
horses? Now there's old Dobbin would have been able
to do light work all summer if he had not been over-
worked, but he is not fit for any work now."

"Yes; an' I'd get rid of him if it wasn't for Mary.
I don't believe in keeping useless animals just out of
sympathy."

"Oh! come now; you don't think God gave man
dominion over the lower animals just that we might
tyrannize over them, and abuse them? There is no
record of any crime they ever committed against the
laws of God, or any disobedience to His will that
should lead Him to give man dominion over them as a
means of punishment; but, on the contrary, it seems as
though He has given them to us to be useful to us,
and make our lives happier. There is a limit to our
dominion, and that limit has been exceeded by you, in
the case of old Dobbin, at least. You had long years
of service from him, and he had grown too old for the
work you put on him. The same reason would probably hold good with the other horses, for I think you
have overworked them this spring. I say it in all
kindness to you; but I think you have got into the
habit of looking at things in the wrong light, and
are measuring things by a false standard."

"You may be right about the matter," said Shane; "but I don't see how a man is to get along in the world if he don't push things."

"That depends on what you mean by pushing things, and getting along in the world. If the getting of money is the aim of life it might be to our interest to wring the last pound of strength from our beasts that could be got out of them, but I believe it is a good policy not only to get happiness for ourselves, *but to make them happy too;* and I don't think I ever lost anything by that policy."

"Well, we can't agree on these questions," said Shane, "and what I want to know is if you will help me out a little with my work, when you get your crop in."

"Why, certainly, I am always willing to help a neighbor when he is in trouble. Let me see: the boys will have that lower field broke up by the middle of the week, and then I will send you one team on one condition, neighbor Shane."

"What is that?" asked Shane.

"That you will apply my principles in regard to the lower animals to my horses. That you will treat them as kindly as I would treat them, and be as merciful to them as you would to me, if I went over to help you."

"I agree to that," said Shane, "an' appreciate your kindness, I am sure."

Shane took his departure and went on to Abner Smith's, who lived on the next farm. Abner Smith was a bluff old fellow who always spoke his mind, and was always free to criticise anything that did not suit him, but his criticisms always had a ring of sincerity, as being the result of honest conviction. Justice to all things, both man and beast, was the ruling principle of his life. Shane's errand here was the same as at Tracy's, and he related his troubles and asked for the use of a team in getting his corn planted.

"Well, I'm always neighborly," said Smith, "an' I think I can spare you a team by the middle of the week, an' I'll send my boy John along to drive it for you."

"That is not necessary," said Shane; "I have plenty of hands. What I want is horses; Tom can drive the team, if you will let me have it."

"I'd rather my boy John would go along with the team," said Smith. "It shan't cost you nothin'. You see the team is used to John, an' then they do say that you are a hard man on hosses, neighbor Shane, an' mine ain't used to bein' ill treated."

"Well, suit yourself about that. By the way, I'll send Tom over to work in John's place, if you insist on sending John with the team."

"That's fair," said Smith. "If you don't need the boy, just send him over an' I'll find work for him."

Farmer Shane returned home feeling more cheerful than he had for some days; but he didn't feel right about the way Tracy and Smith had talked about his treatment of his horses and other animals.

"The idea," he soliloquized, "that I don't know as much about how to use a horse as Abner Smith. Why, I've owned two horses to his one, an' have wore out more horses than he ever owned. I'd get more work out of the horses if he'd let Tom drive 'em, but then I'll have to do the best I can. An' then there's Tracy's horses; I'll use them myself, an' may be John will get ashamed of himself if he don't do as much as I do with Tracy's team; but then I promised Tracy that I wouldn't use his team hard, an' if I did he would never forgive me. John would just be mean enough to go right away an' tell Tracy if I did get a full day's work out of 'em. Well, I'll just have to do the best I can, but I do hate to have to work with people who have such cranky notions. It's strange they can't see that it pays better to work a horse for all there is in him, an' when he's wore out shoot him or give him away. I tell you time is worth more than horse flesh."

Such were the thoughts of a man who was intent on money getting. He forgot that the same God who created him created the lower animals, and that the dominion God gave him over them was a trust to be executed mercifully.

CHAPTER VII.

HE days went by, and Tracy and Smith sent their teams, and the work went merrily on at the Shane farm, and it looked like the corn would be planted in pretty good time yet. Shane's horses were not improving in appearance any, and he had spent the price of a horse in fees to Hodges to treat them. He hoped to get them cured by the time the corn was ready for the cultivator, but the first thing was to get the corn planted.

The work went steadily on, and by the middle of the next week the last hill was in the ground, and Shane was astonished at the amount of work that could be done by two teams, when they were worked according to Tracy's and Smith's plans; for he had kept his promise to Tracy to treat the team well. He had given them proper rest during the day, proper care at night, and had worked them a reasonable number of hours. He remarked that " Smith an' Tracy had two mighty good teams. They just go right along an' do what they are told to do without any fuss or trouble." Yet he could not understand that it was the kind treatment that these horses received that made them work so cheerfully.

" There's an awful sight o' grubworms in this soil,"

said John Smith, as he and Shane were breaking up the ground for corn. "If them blackbirds that's a hangin' around in the woods would come down an' pick 'em up it would be many a dollar in your pocket."

"I ain't got any use for blackbirds," said Shane. "The pesky things will be around when the corn's planted to pull it up. I'd rather take my chances agin the worms than the birds. If I had a gun, I'd start them black rascals out of there."

"They'll pick up a sight of worms if you'll let 'em," said John. "Father don't allow us to kill birds. He says they more than pay their way."

"Maybe they do for some people, but they don't for me," said Shane.

The birds were confining their work to the fields, and were not seen about the house. This was observed soonest by Edith, who was very fond of birds.

"How strange it is, mamma, that there are no birds this summer," said Edith.

"I have noticed it," said Mrs. Shane. "Perhaps they have not come yet."

"Oh! yes they have," said Edith, "there's just lots of them over at Tracy's, and lots of nests. I don't see why they don't build any nests here. It seems so lonesome here without them. I think papa and Tom are cruel to shoot them and drive them away, and I told papa so."

"Don't worry your papa any more than you can help, Edie," said Mrs. Shane. "He has had a great deal of trouble this spring."

"Well, mamma, don't you think he has brought a great deal of this trouble on himself?"

"Perhaps so, Edie; but your papa has ideas about things that are different from ours. He looks at everything from a money point of view."

"I don't think that people who look at things only from a money point of view," said Edith, "get much happiness."

"Your papa is doing what he thinks is for the best, and is looking ahead to save up something for you and Tom."

"Well, I don't want him to make himself miserable all his life to save up money for me. *I would rather be poor and be happy, and have people and animals and birds to love me.* If papa would read the books I borrowed from Cora Tracy he would find out that birds are useful, and instead of trying to kill them and drive them away, he would be glad to have them come."

"Your papa has so many cares that he don't have time to read," said Mrs. Shane.

Edith sat for some time in silence, gazing out over the fields, and up in the blue sky.

"It seems to me like something dreadful is going to happen," she said. "Everything seems so gloomy around here; it doesn't seem like the same place."

"The bad luck your papa has had this spring makes us all feel down-hearted. Perhaps it is all for the best, and we can only hope that it will come out all right."

"I don't think it will come out all right," said Edith. "I don't think papa is doing right to drive away the birds, and work the horses to death; and Mr. Tracy thinks the same thing, for Cora told me so, and I'm going to have a talk with papa about it."

"It is quite useless to annoy him about it," said Mrs. Shane. "His mind is made up, and he will not change it."

This reply did not settle the matter with Edith, for she was determined to talk with her father about the matter, but she did not expect the opportunity to come in the manner it did.

The days slipped by and the corn was coming up, but the difficulties on the Shane farm had not improved any. The horses were still not fit for use, and Hodges could not tell when they would be.

"I don't believe there's anything the matter with that bay Dick," said Shane, "and I'm not going to fool with him any longer. He eats as hearty as ever, and I saw him down in the pasture trotting around as limber as any horse. I'm goin' to hitch him up an' make him work or break his neck. Here's the corn comin' up an' some of the horses have got to go in the field pretty soon."

Having come to this conclusion, he said he would hitch Dick up to the cart and drive him to town, and see if he couldn't limber him up under the whip.

"Do be careful," said Mrs. Shane, "you know that horse has a bad temper."

"Oh! I guess Dick knows me by this time, and he knows I won't stand any nonsense. If he's as lame as he pretends to be, it won't be much trouble to handle him."

Accordingly the harness was put on Dick, and he was hitched to the cart. He stumbled around like a very lame horse, and made a very bad show of getting along. No one but Shane would have undertaken to drive him in the condition he appeared to be in.

"Poor Dick," said Edith, as Shane stopped at the house; "I don't think papa ought to drive him when he is so lame," and she patted his neck and smoothed out his long mane. "Don't drive him hard, papa," she continued, "and I'm sure he'll do the best he can."

Shane made no reply, but drove away toward town. The drive to town and return was a slow one, for even Shane's hard heart would not permit him to drive a lame horse out of a walk. Shane was rather proud of the fact that he had succeeded in driving Dick, and said that all the horse needed was exercise, and he would be at work in a few days. He thought, perhaps, a little exercise would do the rest of the horses good.

The next day Shane proceeded to hitch Dick up again for the purpose of driving him.

"There's no use talkin'," he said to Mike, "I have got to put these horses to work."

"Bether go slow," said Mike, "for if ye put thim sick horses to work too soon ye may have dead ones."

"It is better to have dead horses than useless ones, just standin' round eatin'. A dead horse don't eat anything. It would be money in my pocket if they were all dead," and he gave Dick a sharp cut with the

whip to start him. Dick laid back his ears and hob-
bled away; *but his looks appeared to indicate that a
very little of the whip would limber him up too much
for the good of Shane's health.* Edith being away
there was no one to give the horse a kind word to put
him in a better humor. Shane mounted the cart and
clucked to the horse to start, but Dick stood still.
He had, evidently, made up his mind that he did not
want to work that day. Shane gave him a cut with
the whip, but Dick laid back his ears and shook his
head, as much as to say, "there is trouble coming
for somebody."

"You won't go, eh?" said Shane, and he gave the
horse blow after blow with the whip, almost cutting the
hide open. Dick made a lunge forward, but Shane
pulled with all his strength on the reins, and the hard
bit cut the horse's mouth until it bled, and threw Dick
back on his haunches. The sudden halt threw Shane
forward, and the reins were slackened. This was
Dick's opportunity, and he seized the bit in his teeth,
a trick horses learn when they are abused, and which
they practise to save themselves from punishment by
the bit. Before Shane could recover himself, Dick
had started down the road, forgetting all about his stiff
legs. Shane pulled on the reins until his arms ached,,
but it was the strength of a man against the strength
of a horse. It was the steel bit against the teeth of
the horse, now, and the teeth won. Down the road
they flew with the speed of the wind. They neared
the bend in the road, and Shane knew that the end would

come there, for he never could make the turn without upsetting the cart, but he was helpless. Straight at the fence went Dick, paying no attention to the turn of the road, and with a bound he went over, and the cart was smashed to splinters. Shane lay beside the road unconscious, and to all appearance dead.

Dick kicked himself free from the harness and sped across the field, thankful that he, had the privilege to use his legs once more. Shane had spent his life among horses, but had never learned until now that he could not subdue a high-spirited horse by force.

Mrs. Shane had seen the horse start and feared the result. An elevation in the road had cut off her view, after the horse had passed down the road a few rods, and she knew nothing of the result. She called Mike and Tom from the barn and told them what had occurred.

"Oh! that's all right, mother; I guess father can manage him, as lame as he is," said Tom. "He won't run very far before he will get tired."

"Begorra, I'm not so sure of that," said Mike; "it's a fiery temper the horse has, an' whin his blood's up he's hard to manage."

"I would rather you would go after him and see if anything has happened," said Mrs. Shane.

"Why, how useless that would be, mother; there ain't a horse on the farm we could drive, an' we couldn't catch him on foot."

"I shall not rest until I know," said Mrs. Shane.

"Don't worry about that. Father knows too much

about horses to let Dick get away from him that way," said Tom. "Come, Mike, let's go back to work."

Shane still lay beside the road unconscious. He had tried to manage the horse by brute force, and here was the result—the horse prancing over the field, exulting in his freedom, and the man lying unconscious beside the road. The horse had not expended a tithe of his strength, and the man was as helpless as the dead.

At the time of the accident Edith was visiting Cora Tracy, and in the afternoon Mr. Tracy had occasion to hitch up his wagon and drive down the road on an errand to another farm, and as he was going by the Shane farm he told Edith she could ride with him. She gladly accepted his invitation, for it would save her a long walk.

"I always like to ride behind your horses," said Edith, as they drove along; "they look so happy and contented."

"That's the way I want them to be," said Mr. Tracy. "They deserve to be happy just as much as I do, or any of my family."

"Do you think animals know anything about happiness or unhappiness?" said Edith; "that is, I mean do they know when we love them, and can they love us in return?"

"That is a hard question to answer," said Tracy; "but I think their actions indicate that they appreciate love and kindness as much as a human being does; but whether they understand such things as we do or not, I cannot tell. I have always made it a rule to treat them as though they did. This is especially the case with horses and dogs. I find that I can get much better service out of them by treating them kindly; and then I feel better myself when I have treated all the brute creation fairly, and have dealt justly by them."

"I wish papa would look at things as you do, and would take more interest in the welfare of his dumb animals," said Edith.

"I should think a good little teacher like you could teach him something about such things," said Tracy.

"He won't listen to me," said Edith. "He says I am too young to know much about such things."

"Why, how is this?" exclaimed Tracy, as they passed along the road in the vicinity of the wreck, and saw Dick over in the field. "Here is a horse running loose with a bridle on and part of the harness. Why, it looks like "—he paused in his remark, for he recognized the horse as Mr. Shane's.

"It looks like Dick," said Edith, taking up the sentence and finishing it for him; "but it can't be, for Dick is lame and this horse is not."

"It looks like some one has been in trouble, but I don't see any indications of it on the road. That is one way that high-spirited horses have of retaliating for ill-usage on the part of their masters," he continued, as they drove along the road. On nearing the turn of the road he saw evidences of the wreck made by Dick; but Edith's bright eyes had seen it before he did.

"Oh! Mr. Tracy, there has been a runaway, and there is a man lying beside the road. Oh! I know it must be papa. Do please drive faster and let us see."

Mr. Tracy needed no urging on this point, for he had already started his horses into a trot. As they neared the place the cause of the trouble was apparent. Edith leaped from the wagon and was at her father's side in a moment.

"Oh! dear, dear papa, speak to me," she sobbed, as she lifted his head in her arms. "Oh! Mr. Tracy, is he dead?" she asked, between her sobs.

"He is not dead, my dear girl, but very badly injured, I am afraid," he answered. "Can you stay here with him until I go for assistance?"

"No, no, don't go away; I can help you lift him in the wagon and we will take him home."

"Why, my dear girl, you have not strength to help me lift him."

"Oh! yes I have, Mr. Tracy; I am strong. Come, let me help."

"Well, if you insist, we will try it," he said; and they lifted him up and succeeded in getting him into the wagon, and drove as rapidly as possible to the Shane farm. When they arrived Edith hastened to the house and met her mother on the porch. Edith's swollen eyes told the whole story to Mrs. Shane, and she clasped her daughter in her arms and sobbed: "Is he dead, Edie? is he dead?"

"No, mamma; only hurt," she replied, trying to keep up a stout heart.

Mrs. Shane hastened out to the wagon, and Edith hurried away in search of Tom and Mike, who came and carried Mr. Shane into the house. Mr. Tracy immediately went for the doctor.

"Now, Jerry and Tom, you'll have to trot," he said to his horses, as he touched them lightly with the whip. "It's a case of life and death, old boys, so skip along." And the good horses skimmed over the ground in the best of humor, and soon returned with the doctor.

On examination Shane was found to have a broken leg, and a contusion on the head. He remained in a semi-unconscious condition for the rest of the day. On the following morning he rallied, but had no recollection of the accident until Mrs. Shane explained the matter to him. The bitterest pang to him now was the thought of the two long months of enforced idleness and suffering that were before him.

CHAPTER VIII.

HE story of the accident was soon spread abroad over the farm, and was commented on by all the animals; but the general opinion seemed to be that there would be one person less to abuse them — for a while anyhow.

"I'm sorry Tom wasn't fixed somehow so that he couldn't get out here to beat us," said the cow.

"I don't like that way of doing," said Dobbin to Dick. "You went too far in that matter. Of course everybody will know now that you were playing off, and they may see through the whole thing, and that will result in more violence."

"Well, what is done can't be undone," said Dick, my temper got away with me, and I was tired of shamming. If I had been really lame Shane would have driven me just the same. I was lame for all he knew to the contrary, and when he whipped me I started to run before I had time to think. I knew I might as well make a complete job of it while I was at it; for Shane would know I was shamming anyhow, and I would have to fight it out with him sometime. You see, I had put myself in a position where I had to fight or surrender, and I preferred to fight." ⁵⁹

"It's a very bad piece of business," said Dobbin, "and may make trouble for all of us. You should have kept your temper."

"I tried to and failed, as you see," said Dick. "I have neither your age nor experience in such matters, and make bad breaks sometimes."

"We will have to take some other means of protecting ourselves when Shane gets about again," said Dobbin; "but that won't be for a good many days, so Towser says."

"It's open war with me now," said Dick. "I don't intend that the harness shall go on my back again until this matter is settled. Towser was saying the other day that Shane said if ever we did get able to work he would make us pay dear for our vacation."

The days were long and tedious for Shane as he lay on his bed and brooded over his troubles. To his physical suffering was added the worry about the condition of things on the farm. Mrs. Shane and the children tried to keep all further trouble from him by putting the condition of things in their most favorable light, but he understood his business too thoroughly to be deceived.

"Tom, how long before that corn will be ready for the cultivator?" asked Shane, as Tom was passing through the room.

"I don't know," said Tom, "but when it is the neighbors will all come in and plow it over for you."

"Did the blackbirds take much of it?"

"I don't think they took any of it," said Tom.

"Is it a good stand?"

"It is good enough," replied Tom; "don't worry about that; it will come out all right."

"But I do worry about it. There is something wrong about it; I can tell it by your actions. Come, out with it. One more misfortune won't kill me after I've gone through what I have."

"Well, if you must know," said Tom, "the corn is not a good stand."

"Not a good stand? What is the reason?"

"If you must know about it I might as well tell you all about it. The corn crop is a failure. The worms have taken every stock of it, and it will have to be planted over. Now there ain't any use to worry over it, for Mr. Tracy said that the neighbors would come in and plow up the ground and replant it; but he was afraid you would not raise much corn there on account of the worms."

"Was Tracy's corn destroyed by the worms?"

'No."

"Nor Smith's?"

"No."

"Nor anybody's else?"

"Nobody's around here."

"Then fate is agin me, an' I give up the fight," said Shane.

"Mr. Tracy says there is something peculiar about your corn, an' he says he can't account for it unless it is because there ain't no birds here to take the worms. Mother an' Edie have been talkin' about there bein' no birds here; but I never noticed it particular till Tracy

spoke about it. But I don't believe that had anything
to do with it."

"I don't go nothin' on them foolish notions of his,"
said Shane; "but it does look like there's a kind of
a fate follerin' me this spring."

"Well, don't worry over it, an' we'll plant it over
again, an' may be it will come out all right in the
end."

"There'll be nothin' in it this year. If the worms
took it once they'll take it again, an' we'll get nothin'
out of the corn crop this year."

Tom left Shane more despondent than ever, and he
spent the remainder of the day in a very bad mood.
As the shades of evening crept around him he felt the
burden of his misfortunes more severely than ever.
This, in connection with his broken limb, was more than
he could bear, and caused him to groan aloud. The
sound reached Edith, who sat in the adjoining room.
She crept silently into his room and approached his
bed.

"Poor papa, are you suffering much?" she asked.

"Oh! yes, my girl; it seems like everything is
goin' to ruin."

"Why, papa, how you talk," and she knelt down
by his bedside. "Haven't you a good home, and a
loving family, and kind neighbors?"

"Yes, yes, I know; but then there'll be nothin'
made on the farm this year."

"What if there isn't; we will be just as happy."

"You don't understand, girl; you are not old enough
to understand these things."

"Yes; but I do understand them, papa. I'm seventeen, and I know that you have been wearing out your life trying to lay by money and buy more land. It isn't making us any happier, but instead it is making you and all of us unhappy; and papa you are not so kind as you used to be. You don't love us like you did when I was a little girl."

"Not love you, Edie? why, of course I do. It is for you I am trying to save up money. What better proof do you want of my love?"

"Why, I want a little of this kind of love," and she drew his arm around her neck and kissed him for the first time in years.

This was a new experience for John Shane. The sunlight of such love had not penetrated the dusty recesses of his heart for years, and the dust would have to be cleared away before its genial warmth could reach his soul.

"You are a good daughter, Edie; but you do not understand how necessary it is to have money to get along in the world."

"Oh! yes I do, papa; but I know that money alone will not bring happiness. Let us be happy and not worry about money."

"But how can we live without money, child?"

"Why, you dear old papa, I know you have money enough in the bank to live on for a year if we didn't raise any crops at all."

"And what would you do when that was gone?"

"Why, then you will be well, and the horses will be

well, and we will all go to work with willing hands and
nappy hearts. We will be kind and loving to everybody and everything, and we won't think so much
about making money."

"It sounds good to hear you talk that way, Edie,
but I'm afraid it won't work. A man must look out
an' provide for his own family, for if he don't nobody
will."

"Yes, but if he allows his love for his family to be
driven out by the love of money it seems to me he has
made a bad bargain."

"Well, good night, daughter; you've cheered me
up for a while, anyhow. My misfortunes worry me
most on account of those who are dependent on me. I
want to put them above want."

"There now, papa; no more about that. Let us
encourage love and kindness toward one another and
trust in God. Good night, papa," and she gave him
another kiss and left him.

John Shane was restless; as the hours dragged their
weary length along the loneliness of his situation
pressed itself on him. The conversation with Edith had
aroused the latent energies of his soul, and his heart
yearned for human sympathy. He had lived a lonely
life; his whole soul had been possessed by the one idea
of making money. He did not think that anyone else
was suffering while he was following this false light,
but here was Edith, who had been yearning for her
father's love and had been denied it. Her face
haunted him; her voice was ringing in his ears. Her

words were present in his memory. Her face and voice reminded him of one that he had known long ago — one that he had loved in the years gone by. Who could it be? Why, Mary his wife, of course, whom he had almost forgotten that he ever loved, and when he married her she looked like Edith; why to be sure, and he had almost forgotten it. He felt an indescribable desire to tell her that he loved her yet, and called her to him. When she came and stood beside his bed the vision created by a sick man's fancy faded; for it was not Edith's bright and sunny face that bent over him, but his wife's, and the twenty years that she had toiled by his side had left their mark there. The youth and beauty had gone, and her hair was streaked with gray. It was Mary Shane that stood beside him, and not the vision of Mary Malott that Edith's face had recalled; and he was John Shane again with wrinkled face and stooping shoulders. The vision had faded and the words of affection that his lips should have uttered were left unsaid.

"Did you want something, John?"

"Only a little assistance in changing my position," he replied.

That done, she started away. His conscience smote him and the vision came back. He recalled her and she returned to his bedside.

"What is it, John?" she inquired.

"I am lonely to-night," he replied; "can't you sit with me a while?"

"Why, yes: all night if you need me."

She sat down by him, and he told her how he was beginning to see that his life was not what it should be. That he had neglected his duty as a husband and father, and had lived too much alone, and that henceforth he wanted to take his family more into his confidence. He would have told her that he loved her as of yore, but it had been so long since he had spoken such words of affection to her that the words came but awkwardly to his lips, and he left them unspoken. She replied, with tears in her eyes, that she knew that their thoughts had been drifting apart, and she hailed with joy the dawn of a brighter day, when their lives would flow in the same channel.

Soothed by these thoughts he soon fell asleep, and his tired and worn out wife retired to rest, hoping that the future might not dispel the bright hopes raised that night.

CHAPTER IX.

HE thoughts of the night vanished with the gleams of the rising sun, and the good resolutions that John Shane had made in his conversation with his wife were soon forgotten. The coming of day always meant more to him, and the habit of being up with the sun to engage in his daily toil was of such a fixed character that it angered him to think that he was confined to his bed. Edith's tenderness had led his fancy back twenty years, and he felt again the hopes that had inspired him in former years when Mary Malott became his wife; but the light of day brought back the thoughts of his business, and he was even a little ashamed that he had allowed himself to indulge in such thoughts and words as he did the night before.

The breath of mammon had dissipated the perfume of holiness that had penetrated his heart, and he was again the man of business, blinded by the glitter of gold, unable to see the beauties of a trusting wife and a loving daughter.

Time passed on until two weeks had elapsed since the accident, and the strike was strictly maintained by all the animals. Their lot had been a little easier since

Shane had been confined to the house and they had only Tom to contend with, for Mike was not a hard-hearted fellow, but had only done the bidding of his employer. He never abused the dumb animals on the farm when he could avoid it.

"I'll tell ye, Tom," said Mike, one day, "let's thry a little different plan wid thim horses, an' see if we can't build 'em up a bit."

"Bother the horses; they're goin' to destruction like everything else on the farm," said Tom.

"Be aisy, now, 'til I tell ye how we'll do it. Let's clane out the stables, an' put clane straw in the stalls for beddin'. Thin we'll make a nice warm mash for 'em to ate, an' thrate 'em like gintlemen, begorra, an' see if we can't put some life into 'em."

"You can try it if you want to, but I shan't fool away my time that way," said Tom.

"By your lave I'll thry that same plan mesilf, thin," said Mike.

Mike was as good as his word, and brought the horses up at night, and had bedding of nice clean straw for them to sleep on. He curried, brushed and rubbed them, until their neglected coats began to shine again. He saw that they were properly fed with good whole-some food, and closed the openings in the stable, that the night winds might not blow on them.

"What's up now, do you suppose?" said Dobbin, after Mike had gone away. "This begins to look like things were turning our way."

"I don't like favors coming from the hand of the

enemy," said Dick. "Let's go slow until we find out if there isn't some trick in it."

"Well, no matter what the cause of the change is, I'm going to get all the pleasure I can out of my improved condition for one night, anyhow," said the sorrel horse; and the gray mare said: "Them's my sentiments."

Mike followed up his plan by giving them the same attention the next day, and the horses began to think that a change had come for the better, but Dick maintained that it was because their old enemy Shane was laid up. Mike never was a cruel master, and he thought Mike was taking advantage of his employer's sickness to give them a little better treatment.

"Well, if Mike is going to be fair with us, let's be fair with him," said the sorrel. "I'm kind of tired of playing sick, anyhow."

"I don't object to working for anybody that will treat me fair," said Dick; "and if Mike is going to treat us right I am willing to work."

About this time Mike went up to the house to see Mr. Shane.

"Mornin' to ye, Misther Shane; an' how are ye this mornin'?" said Mike.

"Bad, Mike, still bad," said Shane; "everything is goin' to ruin on the place I suppose."

"Faith now an' they're not. I've been tindin' to thim horses mesilf for a few days; I'm tindin' to 'em rigular, and ye ought to see the improvement in 'em. Why, they'll all be at work again in a few days."

"Well, that's some encouragement anyhow," said Shane. "What are you doing for the horses?"

"I'm just tratin' 'em like gintlemen. *I'm doin' unto thim horses as I would have thim do unto me.* I ain't much of a scholar, and maybe not so good a Christian as I ought to be, but I belave that's a good rule to go by. Just trate 'em kindly an' dacently, an' that's the whole sacret of it all. Just lave me alone wid 'em, an' I'll have 'em at work again in a few days."

Edith came in shortly after Mike took his leave.

"Good morning, Edie; I believe I feel a little better this morning," said Shane.

"I'm glad to hear that," said Edith. "I'll just open the window so that you can see out. I'm afraid mamma is going to be sick; she is scarcely able to be up."

"Why, what is the matter with her?" inquired Shane. He had been so engrossed by his own selfish thoughts that he had not noticed that his wife was wearing out under the increased duties put upon her since his sickness.

Sure enough Mrs. Shane was taken sick that day, and Towser carried the news to the barnyard.

"Well now, that's bad," said Dobbin. "Some one of us will have to go for a doctor."

"I'll go," said Dick.

"I hope they'll take me," said the sorrel. "I am tired of staying at home, anyhow."

Mike was called up to go for a physician. "Time

is money,'' he said; ''an' I'll just take one of these horses. I wonther which one of the lazy rogues I'd bether take.''

Dick whinnied, as much as to say, ''I'll go.''

''Ah! ye rogue, would ye thry yer ould thrick an' run away wid me? But ye're the fastest one of the lot, an' I'll thry ye anyhow.''

He harnessed Dick, and hitched him to the buggy. Once in the highway, Dick skimmed over the ground like a bird and soon brought the physician to Mrs. Shane's bedside.

''It was just a case of overwork and lack of sleep,'' said the physician. ''Too much hard work in the day, and sitting up of nights, and all she needed was complete rest.''

Mr. Tracy came over that day to see Shane.

''Things are worse than ever, now, Neighbor Tracy,'' said Shane, and he related his new misfortune in his wife's sickness. ''Why, I never thought about her overworkin' herself,'' he said.

''Well, if you'll allow me to speak plainly to you, neighbor Shane, you should have seen that your wife was breaking down under the strain of increased duties that have been put upon her since your sickness.''

''I admit it,'' said Shane; ''but I had so many things to think of that I never thought of it.''

''Why, my dear friend, is there anything more important to you than the health and happiness of your family? The happiness of those who are dependent upon you should be the uppermost thought in your mind. The wife who has confided her life to your keeping should be the first in your thoughts."

"I really had not thought about her being over-worked," said Shane.

"You have a false idea of the powers of endurance of both man and beast. There is a limit to the physical endurance of both, which can be and often is exceeded. You have the proof of that statement before you. Your wife is down sick from overwork, and your horses are disabled from the same cause."

"There, I don't agree with you," said Shane. "It's just a streak of bad luck I have struck, and I couldn't help it."

"If you would just stop and reason about the matter you would see it in a different light. I don't want to intrude upon your private affairs, but I feel that it is my duty to present some things to you in the light that I see them, for I think that you are blinded, and do not see things that are to your interest. You have sacrificed your own happiness and that of your family to get money, and what have you got in return? Why, nothing; while I, who have followed the other rule of seeking happiness, have more of this world's wealth than you have, and I do not want to say it with any thought of boasting."

"You always was lucky," said Shane.

"There is no luck about it," said Tracy. "The word of God is true, and if a man tries to follow its teachings I believe he will be prospered."

Edith had come in and sat down by Shane's bed-side, and taken his hand in hers.

"Papa," she said, "I think Mr. Tracy is right, and I wish you would heed his words."

"There is something peculiar about the condition of things here on the farm," continued Tracy, "which I am unable to understand; and while I don't think that God ever singles out one individual on which to inflict punishment, yet it does not seem to me that the situation of things here is a matter of chance. Why, if you have not noticed it I will call your attention to the fact that there is not a bird on your farm."

"Yes, papa; if you will just listen there is not a bird's voice to be heard, and they used to sing so sweetly," said Edith. "It is so lonely without them, and makes me feel like some great misfortune is hanging over us."

"I think my attention had been called to their absence," said Shane; "but I thought I was lucky to get rid of 'em."

"Quite the contrary," said Tracy, "it is the most unfortunate thing that has occurred to you. Those birds that you have been trying to kill all your life, and which you have succeeded in driving away, would have saved your crop, which has been destroyed by worms and insects. Why, there have been hundreds of them in my fields all the spring, and see what a fine prospect I have for a good crop. If you would take time to study these matters you would see that birds are one of the best gifts God has given us. They destroy immense numbers of insects that are injurious to trees and plants, and I think that all the vegetation on your farm shows the absence of what would be your best friends. Whether you drove them away or whether some superior intelligence directed their flight I cannot tell, but they are gone, and your farm is suffering from their absence."

"That is true, papa. The birds were your friends, and you drove them away," said Edith.

"There may be something in that," said Shane, half convinced; "an' I'll think about it."

"God gave us the beasts and birds for our use and benefit. He gave man dominion over them, and he has not withdrawn or changed his law; but he can remove them from our presence, as he has removed the birds from this farm. He can disable the dumb animals so that they cannot work for us, as is the case with your horses, although I think the condition of your horses is the result of overwork. You will have to admit that you have overworked your horses this spring. It is a remarkable fact that they all became afflicted at the same time, and one that I can't understand. You must realize, friend Shane, that horses have a physical construction similar to our own, and that their strength can be overtaxed the same as a man's, and if overwork will break down your wife's health, as you now see that it has, why will it not do the same to a horse?"

"I begin to see that I may have been mistaken in regard to these matters," said Shane, and Edith gave his hand an encouraging clasp.

"Why, kindness goes a long way with dumb brutes

in helping them to bear up under hard work," continued Tracy, "*and I fear that you haven't given your animals the encouragement of kind words even.* Love and kindness are the powers that govern the world. You may control a horse by force for a while, but if he has any spirit it will break out sometime, and the horse by his superior strength will be master, as was the case with Dick when he ran away with you. Mike said he never saw a horse drive nicer than Dick did when he went after the doctor. Why, you wouldn't know your own horses, Shane, since Mike has been applying the 'golden rule' to them, as he says. If they keep on improving they will be at work again in a short time."

"Won't that be nice, papa?" said Edith.

"I just give you these points to think about, and when you get up put them into practice, and see if it don't prove more profitable than the old way. I'll get the neighbors together and we'll replant that corn and see if you can't make a crop yet. I'll send Cora over to help Edie with the work until you can get some one else. So good bye, friend Shane, and don't worry about your business, for your neighbors will help you out."

CHAPTER X.

HANE thought seriously about the conversation he had with Tracy, and came to the conclusion that perhaps he had been following a false light — that he had not gotten as much happiness out of life as he might. He recalled many acts of unkindness towards the wife and daughter who loved him, and he resolved to lead a different life.

While these thoughts were in his mind Edith came into the room and sat down beside him.

"How is your mother now, Edie?" he said.

"I think she is better, papa."

"Edie, I've been thinkin' that I haven't done right by her. I haven't made her life as happy as I might, an' I'm goin' to change things when I get well."

"I'm sure mamma never complains, papa, but we would all be so much happier if you would give us the same love you used to," said Edith, "and give up this struggle for money and try to be happy."

"That's what I'm goin' to do, Edie."

"Oh! papa, I'm so glad," and she put her arms around his neck.

"And, Edie, you spend a good deal of time readin' books; what do you think of Tracy's ideas in regard to animals?"

"They are true, papa, they are true," she said. "God gave us the birds and animals, and I think it is a sin for us to abuse them. He will certainly hold us to account for our treatment of his creatures." Her bowed head bent over his face, and a tear-drop from her eye fell on his cheek. "And oh! papa, if you would be loving and kind, not only to mamma and Tom and me, but to all the living creatures that God has given us, I would love you so much, and we would be so much happier."

"There, now, daughter, don't cry. I believe you are right about it, an' I'm goin' to change things an' try a new way. It may come a little awkward at first, but I think I can get used to it."

"Oh! papa, I'm so glad. I'll go and tell mamma, and it will help her to get well," said Edith.

"Just send Tom in; I want to talk to him awhile," said Shane.

Tom sauntered into his father's room wondering what was up, for he had seen by Edith's face that something important had happened.

"Tom," said Shane, after a pause of a few seconds, "I've come to the conclusion that we haven't been runnin' the farm on the right principle. I know you've been follerin' in my footsteps an' doin' things as I do 'em, which is quite natural for a boy to do; but I guess we've been mistaken in a few things, an' we'll just take a square turn an' make a new start in another direction. There's somethin' wrong on the farm, an' if it's a judgment sent on us for some of our shortcomings, why,

let's try an' git in the right path agin. We'll try kindness toward our dumb animals, an' the birds, an' each
other, an' see if that ain't a better rule to live by."

"I'm agreed to that," said Tom, much to his father's
surprise, "for I've been thinking some that way myself, since Mike has been takin' care of the horses an'
applyin' the 'golden rule' to 'em, as he says. It has
helped 'em more than all of Hodge's doctorin'."

"Well, we'll try the rule of kindness from now on,"
said Shane, and so the matter was settled.

Towser, who had been lying under the window, got
up and capered about the yard for pure joy, and the
next morning, before daybreak, he was out in the
barnyard and had related the whole story of Shane's
new resolutions, which created quite a sensation among
the animals.

"I think we have reason to believe that it is all true,
for we have had much better treatment in the past
week than ever before in our lives," said Dobbin.

"I feel quite well this morning, and if I had a good
feed I think I could pull a plow," said the sorrel.

"Under the circumstances I'm ready to go to work
again," said the gray mare.

"I wish I could lay two eggs to-day," cackled the
hen, and as an evidence of her good intentions she
made a new nest on the barn floor, where Edith could
not help but find it.

Dobbin called another convention of all the birds
and animals for the purpose of declaring the strike
ended, and Towser volunteered to carry the news all

around; and at noon, when they met at the oak tree, there was not one absent. Towser related what he had heard under the window, and they all accepted the matter as a settled fact.

Dobbin declared the strike ended, and requested them all to go to work in good earnest to help Shane out of his troubles. The horses all agreed to go to work the next day. The cow said she would astonish everybody by the amount of milk she would give.

Towser told them that farmer Tracy had promised that the neighbors would come and replant the corn the next day.

"Then I will have a few hundreds of my friends here to kill all the worms in the field if they will let us," said the blackbird, and all the other birds volun-teered their assistance and promised that the farm should be immediately inhabited by an army of birds.

The meeting adjourned sine die, and then there was great rejoicing over the success of the strike.

"Why, there's a robin in the cedar tree," said Edith, in surprise that afternoon. "It seems like a promise of better times to hear its welcome voice. Why, mamma, just listen, there is a host of them coming."

The trees were soon filled with birds of all kinds, which chirped and sang with all their power.

"Papa, just listen to the birds," said Edith, entering her father's room. "Isn't it delightful to have them back again?"

"It does seem more pleasant to have 'em here," said

Shane; "but it's the strangest thing I ever heard of that they'd all come back at once."

"*Perhaps God sent them back on account of your good resolutions to be kind to all his creatures,*" said Edith, and she knelt down by his bedside and put her arms around his neck. "Promise me here in His name, papa, that you will keep that resolution."

"I do," he answered.

"Well, I never seen the like," shouted Tom, as he came bolting into the house. "Them horses are just prancin' an' runnin' all over the pasture, just like they never had anything the matter with 'em. Seems like Mike's treatment was purty good to cure 'em up so soon. I think old Hodges had better take a few lessons from him."

"Yes, and don't forget to take a few lessons yourself, Tom, for you may have to practice in that line. Listen to the birds, too," said Edith.

"By gracious I hadn't noticed 'em. It begins to look like the old place was coming back to itself, don't it?" and he caught her around the waist and whirled her away in a fantastic dance, until she broke loose from him to go to her mother's room with the good news.

In the morning, as Tom went out to the barn he saw three or four cats running about the barn, and picked up a stone to throw at them.

"*Be aisy there, now,*" said Mike; '*it's agin the rules to do that now.*"

"Right you are," said Tom; "but I can't get used to it. What are they doing here, anyhow?"

"Begorra, they're killin' all the rats in the barn, an' the divil a rat can get away from all thim cats."

"Good luck to 'em, then, for the rats were about to take us," said Tom. "How were the horses?"

"Now, look ye, Tom; do ye mind how lame thim horses was?"

"Yes."

"Well, the divil a stiff leg is there among 'em at all, except Dobbin."

"How do you account for it?" asked Tom.

"*It's the tratement I give 'em. I've got a resate for it*, an' it's good for man an' baste, an' ivery other living crayture. Ye'll find it in the Good Book, an' its like this: '*Do thou unto others as thou wouldst have them do unto thee,*' an' *that's a good resate, begorra.*"

"Why, Mike, you're getting poetical."

"Sure an' I'm feelin' poetical, an' if me voice wasn't out of tune I'd sing ye a bit of a song."

"Never mind your voice; give us the song."

"Thin here goes wid a song I composed mesilf to suit the occasion : —

> I'm Michael McCarty,
> So hale and so hearty—
> I work ivery day in the year;
>
> The horses all know me,
> The cattle all show me
> They know they have nothing to fear.
>
> Stan' up for the brutes,
> An' the birds, if it suits
> An' the chickens an' turkeys alone,

For God made 'em all,
'An they came at his call,
An' he gave 'em to man for his own.

We shouldn't abuse 'em,
Nor cruelly use 'em ;
Begorra, I know I am right,

An' before ye shall do it,
I'll have ye to know it,
'Tis Michael M'Carty ye'll fight."

"Bravo! Mike," shouted Edith, who had entered the barn unperceived just as Mike commenced his song.

"Faith, I didn't know I had such an ilegant audience, or sure I'd have been blushin' all the time."

"Quite unnecessary, I am sure," said Edith ; "your audience appreciates your song, and will encore you on the slightest provocation."

"Thin I could only bow me thanks, for sure 'tis the only song I know," said Mike ; "an' 'tis that swate voice of yours we would like to hear, if ye'll be so kind as to sing us a song."

"Oh! excuse me, please," said Edith.

"Oh! come, now," said Tom, "you slipped into our entertainment an' you can't get off so easy. Give us a song or I'll lock you in the barn."

"An' I'll let ye out," said Mike, "but sing us a song, because ye're a nice, swate little girl an' want to plaze yer frinds."

"Well, if I must, I will," said Edith, and she sang the following lines to the tune of "Auld Lang Syne":

> This earth was once inhabited
>   By birds and beasts alone,
> Who held dominion over it,
>   And ruled it as their own
>
> 'Till God created man and made
>   Him ruler over all;
> And then the birds and beasts at once
>   Fell prostrate at his call.
>
> Restrain the hand in anger raised
>   To treat them cruelly;
> He gave them as a precious gift
>   In trust to you and me.
>
> He gave them for our benefit,
>   And not to be abused,
> And he who violates that trust
>   Stands before God accused.
>
> Then do to them as thou wouldst wish
>   That they should do to thee,
> And do not violate the trust
>   God placed in you and me.

"Thank ye, Miss Edith, thank ye; it's a beautiful song, it is. I'm not much at the singin' like ye are; but I can be doin' them things ye sung about, an' I'll not be forgettin' 'em soon."

"Now, come on, bye, an' let's be gettin' ready for the work. The neighbors will all be comin' in purty soon to replant the corn, an' won't they be surprised to see us wid a good team goin' out into the field to work? Begorra they will."

CHAPTER XI.

OHN Shane's neighbors came promptly to his assistance, as they always do in farming communities. They came with their teams and tools, prepared to put in the corn, and the work of plowing up the ground and replanting the corn went merrily on. The birds came and did their share of the work. They followed the plows all day long and caught every worm that came to view. The men plowed the ground and harrowed it and stirred it all they could, so that the birds might get the worms. Shane's horses went to the work with a will, and did as much as any team on the farm. It was a glorious day, and a jollier crowd of men never got together than these same farmers. They felt happy because they were doing a generous deed, and they worked with a will until noon. The dinner bell rang and they went to the house to meet a fresh surprise. Every man's wife and daughter was there, and they had spread a long table under the trees, and put on it a feast that would tempt the appetite of an epicure.

They had gotten Mr. Shane in a chair and placed him at the window where he could see it all; and Mrs. Shane sat by his side, husband and wife, happier than they had been in many years. What a great feast that was there under the trees. What appetites the men had, and how eager the women were to satisfy them. They laughed and joked and ate, and there never was such a jolly time as they had on the Shane farm.

They worked all day and came back the next day, and worked until every hill of corn was planted again. The next day the rain fell and moistened the ground, and the sun came out and warmed it, and the corn sprouted and grew, and there was a great prospect for the future. 'Tis true the worms took some of it, but they had put an extra grain in each hill for the worms. The birds could not get all the worms, but they got most of them. The Shane farm was getting in accord with the plan of the universe, and prosperity was smiling on it.

Shane felt that he was in the right path now, and he studiously followed it. During the time he was confined to the house with his broken limb Edith had induced him to read the books loaned her by Cora Tracy, which treat of animals and birds and their uses.

In a few more weeks Shane recovered so much that he could walk about the farm on crutches. He could not help but mark the difference in the appearance of things. There was a look of content about everything.

The first time he went to the barn Dick came up to him, and putting out his nose touched Shane's hand.

"I actually believe the horse is trying to ask my pardon," said Shane. "It would be more proper for me to ask his pardon for mistreating him so long."

He patted Dick's neck and said, "I think we understand each other now, old fellow."

"I tell ye, Misther Shane, I never see horses work nicer than these same horses of yours," said Mike. "I think we'll have Dobbin prancin' around again purty soon."

"Poor old Dobbin. I'm afraid he'll not get much more enjoyment out of life, but he shall have an easy time of it as long as he lives."

But ere another year had gone by old Dobbin found a resting place beneath the sod, and the question was again asked, "*Who knoweth that the spirit of man goeth upward and the spirit of the beast goeth downward?*" God created him and made him subject to the will of man, and in the end God took him. The part that was mortal went back to the earth. If there was any immortal element in him God took it and knows what to do with it.

The work went on merrily on the Shane farm, and everything prospered. The birds did their duty nobly, and the crops were looking splendidly. Shane completely recovered from his broken limb, and people remarked that Shane didn't seem like the same man he used to be. He had learned that the birds were his friends; he had watched them in their work during the summer, and noticed how diligent they were in searching for insects. They took a few cherries and berries, it is true, but when he came to estimate the value of the fruit taken he saw that its value was greatly overbalanced by the benefits he received.

He had been accustomed to employing men to work for him, and he estimated the wages he would have to pay these men in comparison with the profits he could make out of their labor. If the balance was on his side of the account he employed them, and if not he didn't. He estimated the same way in regard to the birds.

The corn crop destroyed by the worms in the spring was worth more than all the fruit on his farm, and the second crop planted, which he believed now was saved by the birds, was worth all the fruit he would raise in several years. So he reasoned the matter with Edith.

"But, papa," she said, "isn't there something grander and nobler in this question than the mere money side of it?"

"Oh! yes, Edie; I see that side of the question, too. *I recognize now that they are God's creatures, sent for our benefit, and that as he has given them to us he can take them away.*"

"And isn't there something more than that?" asked Edith.

"Yes; I appreciate their sweet songs now as I never did before. There are a great many beauties in nature that I never saw before. I begin to appreciate the gentleness and docility of our domestic animals. I don't blame Dick for running away with me; he only retaliated for the ill-usage I had given him. I do not intend that any dumb animal shall ever be mistreated on this farm again."

"Faith an' I don't think there's iny body on the farm now that wants to mistrate 'em, Misther Shane," said Mike, who had come in with Tom.

"I can trust you, Mike, for you always was opposed to mistreating the animals, but I didn't know but what Tom might have some of the old ideas yet," said Shane.

"Niver ye fear for that bye, Misther Shane. Begorra, he's a bigger crank than Misther Tracy himsilf, *an' I think it's a young leedy of that name that's having a dale of influence wid 'im on thim points, eh?*" and he gave Tom a vigorous poke in the ribs.

"Oh! shut up," said Tom, "that rattle-clap tongue of yours is always clattering about something."

"All right, me bye, 'tis Michael McCarty knows a thing or two, an' he has the tongue to tell ye of it wid Arrah, I've been kapin' me two eyes open mesilf, this summer, an' I've changed the song I sung ye in the spring like this : —

> Tom Shane's a bye of some good sinse —
>   He's goin' to use it all,
> An' from the looks of things just now,
>   Bedad he'll marry this fall,
>   Bedad he'll marry this fall,
> An' from the looks of things just now,
>   Bedad he'll marry this fall.

That is, ye know, if he can get his feyther's consint."

The laugh was at Tom's expense, and they retired in good humor.

"Mike's surmise was correct, for Tom Shane and

Cora Tracy were married the next winter, and it was her influence which had worked a change in Tom's thoughts and actions towards the lower animals.

The summer wore away and the winter was coming on. Shane's corn crop was in the crib, and had yielded far beyond his expectations, and his horses were sleek and fat and happy. He had brought the carpenters up from the village to repair the stables so that no cold blasts of winter winds would blow on his horses. He had bought blankets for his horses — something he had never done before.

The cold weather came on apace, and about the middle of November there came a snowstorm. The pitiless blasts of wind drove the snow in blinding sheets across the fields, and made the warm fireside in the Shane household seem doubly dear to all who love a home.

Edith was standing at the window watching the gusts of wind drive the snow about.

"Oh! say, papa, there is some animal down at the gate," said Edith. "Are any of ours out?"

"I think not," he said, coming to the window. "Ah! it is that old mule that has been living in the highway all summer."

"Whom does it belong to, papa?"

"I don't know; it is a stray. It looks like a shame to let the old fellow stand out there and starve," said Shane.

"Let's take him in until the storm is over, anyhow," said Edith.

"Well, it shall be done," said Shane. "Tom, you an' Mike go an' put that old mule in the back stall an' give him something to eat."

The mule, much to his astonishment, was driven into the stable and put in a warm stall. Corn and hay were put in for him to eat, and he proceeded to fill his empty stomach without any thought of saying grace.

"How is this?" he cried to Dobbin; "there's been some changes since I was here before."

"Well, I should say so," said Dobbin. "We have everything heart could wish for now."

"Well, I'm glad to hear that," said the mule, "and if I can get a job here I'm going to stay."

"I hope you will," said Dobbin, "for we all feel kindly towards you for instructing us how to carry on the strike."

"Well, there's one mule thoroughly surprised," said Tom, after they had returned to the house. "I never saw an animal look so surprised as he did when we put him in the stable; an' the way he shook the snow off his old faded hide and went for that corn was a sight to see."

"Well, it won't cost much to keep him, an' I guess we'll just let him stay this winter," and the mule got his job.

"*That's right, Misther Shane, an' the good God will give ye cridit for it in the nixt world,*" said Mike.

"And all God-fearing people will give you credit for it in this world," said Mrs. Shane.

"The satisfaction of a good easy conscience is all the reward I want," said Shane.

Prosperity smiles on John Shane's farm, and no consideration would induce him to return to the old way of living. *May the time soon come when all men will recognize the fact that the laws of God and humanity require us to be merciful to the dumb animals, and to grant the same justice and mercy to them we would ask for ourselves.*